LUCILLE CAMPS IN

by Kathryn Lasky   illustrated by Marylin Hafner

Alfred A. Knopf ⤳ New York

For Natalie
—K.L.

For Marc, Laurie, and Eliza…dear friends
—M.H.

THIS IS A BORZOI BOOK PUBLISHED BY ALFRED A. KNOPF

Text copyright © 2003 by Kathryn Lasky
Illustrations copyright © 2003 by Marylin Hafner

Published in the United States by Alfred A. Knopf, an imprint of Random House Children's Books,
a division of Random House, Inc., New York, and simultaneously in Canada by Random House of Canada Limited, Toronto.
Distributed by Random House, Inc., New York.
KNOPF, BORZOI BOOKS, and the colophon are registered trademarks of Random House, Inc.

www.randomhouse.com/kids

Library of Congress Cataloging-in-Publication Data
Lasky, Kathryn
Lucille camps in / by Kathryn Lasky ; illustrated by Marylin Hafner. — 1st ed.
p. cm.
SUMMARY: When Lucille is upset that she cannot go camping with her father and older siblings, she and her mother decide to go
camping inside the house.
[1. Camping—Fiction. 2. Family life—Fiction. 3. Pigs—Fiction.] I. Hafner, Marylin, ill. II. Title.

PZ7.L3274 Lp 2003
[E]—dc21   2002027493
ISBN 0-517-80041-1 (trade) — ISBN 0-517-80042-X (lib. bdg.)
Printed in the United States of America
May 2003
10   9   8   7   6   5   4   3   2   1
First Edition

"Me too!" shouted Lucille.
Her father was taking her older
brother and sister camping.

"You'll be in the way," said Franklin.

"Will not!" said Lucille.

"You're too young to go camping," said Frances.

"Am not!" said Lucille.

"Remember the marshmallows for roasting, Dad,"
Franklin said.

"Look at my new flashlight," Frances said. "Just like
Daddy's. A high and low beam."

"Me too! No fair!" Lucille wailed, stomped her feet,
and jumped up and down.

"She's doing the Me Too dance," Frances whispered.

"Now, Lucille," said her dad. "Let's be a good sport.
How about I give you my flashlight?"

"High and low beams?" Lucille asked.

"Right," her father said.

HERE ARE
THE BROWNIES
AND THE
GUM BALLS.

The flashlight made Lucille feel better for
a little while, but she was sad again as she
watched them get ready to leave. Lucille
forgot all about the flashlight.

"Have a good time," called their mother. "Say good-bye, Lucille."

Lucille waved good-bye and said, "I don't like any of you."

Lucille cried. When she stopped crying, she sulked.

"Do you want to play with makeup, Lucille, and put on my new lipstick?" her mother asked.

"Do you want to sit on my lap and send an e-mail to Grandma?"

"Do you want to make cookies,
Lucille? You can lick the bowl."
"Maybe," said Lucille.

Lucille's mom made the cookies. Lucille
licked the bowl. Then she napped while the
cookies baked.

Lucille dreamed of knapsacks and flashlights and tents and roasting marshmallows over a fire. When she woke up, it was almost dark. Dark enough for a flashlight. She turned it on—high beam, then low beam, then high again. She had an idea.

She went to her bed and got
a pillowcase. She filled it with
her favorite things.

"My knapsack!" she said, and swung it over her shoulder.
She looked at her plaid bedspread. "Tent," she whispered.

She pulled it off the bed and dragged it down the stairs.

"Lucille, what are you doing?" her mother asked.

"Camping in!" Lucille answered. "This is the tent."

"What a good idea. And I have some extra sleeping bags.
And even a canteen. Can I share the tent with you?"

"Sure," said Lucille. "Let's put it up together."

Lucille and her mom spread the tent over three chairs
and a stepladder. It was cozy inside.

"How about I start a fire?" said her mom. "We can roast
marshmallows."

"Dessert before dinner?" Lucille could hardly believe it.

So they roasted marshmallows and had apples, raisins, cheese sandwiches, peanut butter and crackers, and Lucille's favorite: Mom's chocolate chip cookies.

After dinner they crawled into the tent and snuggled down in their sleeping bags. They left a tent flap open so they could see the moon and the stars through the window.

Lucille's mother pointed to the star pictures in the sky. "See the Great Bear? There it is. See the swan? There's its wing."

Then Lucille told her mother a moon story.
"See that face in the moon?"

"The man in the moon," said her mother.
"Well," said Lucille, "there are really two faces."
"Two faces?" asked her mom.

"Yep." Lucille spoke very softly. "A mommy and a little girl, and they are floating over the whole wide world."

Lucille snuggled close to her mother,
and soon they were both asleep.

"Uh-oh!" Lucille said the next morning as she watched her mother try to toast a bagel in the fireplace. "Marshmallows work better, Mommy."

"They sure do." So they ate marshmallows and apples and cheese and red Jell-O for breakfast.

Lucille decided to draw pictures of everything she
and her mom had done camping in.

Just as she finished her
moon drawing, they heard the
car drive up. Lucille's dad
called out, "We're home!"

"How was your camping trip?" asked Lucille's mother.

"I caught a fish for dinner," Franklin said.

"I have twenty-two mosquito bites," said Frances.

"I don't have any," said Franklin.

"I caught a frog," said Frances. "But I let it go."

"Dad forgot the dessert," said Franklin.

"Who wants a marshmallow?" asked Lucille.

"Next year, you'll be old enough to go
camping, Lucille," said her father.

"Maybe," Lucille said, and smiled.